For Miles

MG

For my mother, Feng Ying

YR

First US edition 2022
First published by Otter-Barry Books, Little Orchard (Great Britain) 2021

Library of Congress Catalog Card Number pending
ISBN 978-1-5362-2315-6

22 23 24 25 26 27 TLF 10 9 8 7 6 5 4 3 2 1

Printed in Dongguan, Guangdong, China

This book was typeset in Granjon.
The illustrations were done in cut paper and pencil.

Candlewick Press
99 Dover Street
Somerville, Massachusetts 02144

www.candlewick.com

Shu Lin's Grandpa

Matt Goodfellow

illustrated by Yu Rong

CANDLEWICK PRESS

When Shu Lin came to our school, she wore yellow rain boots and a pink coat.

She didn't speak English very well.

At recess, some of the girls buzzed around Shu Lin, trying to get her to skip rope with them. But she stood on her own at the edge of the playground.

"What's up with her?" Barney said.

At lunchtime, Shu Lin sat alone at a table in the cafeteria.
She laid out little boxes of brightly colored food.
We'd never seen anything like it.

"How can she eat that?" Barney said.

On the way home, I remembered
my first day at school, when I had to
stand in front of my new class.

"Let's make Dylan feel at home,"
my teacher had said.

But I hadn't
felt at home.
I wondered if
that's how Shu Lin felt.

One day, Miss Rogers said that
Shu Lin's grandpa was coming
to show our class his paintings.

We sat in silence . . .

"What's the point if he can't even speak English?" Barney said.

Shu Lin's grandpa sat down, opened his satchel,
and passed his paintings around.

Barney dipped his fingers into the water pot.
Anything I tried ended up a mess of splotches.

We helped Miss Rogers push back our desks and place big sheets of white paper on the floor. Paintbrushes and ink were passed out so we could have a go at some paintings of our own.

Shu Lin's grandpa watched us carefully as we
admired his paintings, but he never even spoke.

When it was time to leave,
he just packed up his paintings,
gave Shu Lin a kiss—
and was gone.

Shu Lin sat down next to us.

She smiled and showed us how to hold
the paintbrush properly. How to get
smooth strokes for the dragon's scales.

"Thanks," I said as we were putting
on our coats. "Thanks very much."

Shu Lin let out a little laugh.
"Welcome," she said.

Even Barney smiled.
"Nice one, Shu Lin," he told her.

That night, lying in bed, I closed my eyes and heard wind chimes in bamboo forests. I watched thin smoke wisps melt into stars, and somewhere, deep in the distance of my dreams, I fire-danced with dragons.